*Kevin J. Kennedy
Presents
Horror Tales from
Scotland*

Horror Tales from Scotland © 2025 Kevin J. Kennedy

Edited by Ann Keeran & Kevin J. Kennedy

Cover design by Michael Bray

All rights reserved. No part of this publication may be reproduced, distributed, or transmitted in any form or by any means, including photocopying, recording, or other electronic or mechanical methods, without the prior written permission of the publisher, except in the case of brief quotations embodied in critical reviews and certain other non-commercial uses permitted by copyright law.

First Printing, 2025

Other Books by KJK Publishing

Collections
Dark Thoughts
Vampiro and Other Strange Tales of the Macabre
Merry Fuckin' Christmas and Other Yuletide Shit!
The A to Z of Horror

Anthologies
Collected Christmas Horror Shorts
Collected Easter Horror Shorts
Collected Halloween Horror Shorts
Collected Christmas Horror Shorts 2
Collected Christmas Horror Shorts 3
Collected Christmas Horror Shorts 4
The Best of Indie Horror
The Best of Indie Horror Christmas Edition
100 Word Horrors
100 Word Horrors 2
100 Word Horrors 3
100 Word Horrors 4
Carnival of Horror
Inside the Indie Horror World
Vampires
Werewolves
The Horror Collection: Gold Edition
The Horror Collection: Black Edition
The Horror Collection: Purple Edition
The Horror Collection: White Edition
The Horror Collection: Silver Edition
The Horror Collection: Pink Edition

The Horror Collection: Emerald Edition
The Horror Collection: Pumpkin Edition
The Horror Collection: Yellow Edition
The Horror Collection: Ruby Edition
The Horror Collection: Extreme Edition
The Horror Collection: Nightmare Edition
The Horror Collection: Sapphire Edition
The Horror Collection: The Lost Edition
The Horror Collection: LGBTQIA+ Edition
The Horror Collection: Monster Edition
The Horror Collection: Sci-Fi Edition
The Horror Collection: Turquoise Edition
The Horror Collection: Topaz Edition
The Horror Collection: Splatterpunk Dreams
The Horror Collection: Morte Edition
The Horror Collection: Crystal Edition

Novels and Novellas

Pandemonium by J.C. Michael
You Only Get One Shot by Kevin J. Kennedy & J.C. Michael
Screechers by Kevin J. Kennedy & Christina Bergling
Stitches by Steven Stacy & Kevin J. Kennedy
Halloween Land by Kevin J. Kennedy
The Clown by Kevin J. Kennedy

Foreword

When I found out that I was going to be at Horror Con Scotland with three other Scottish horror authors and that they had put our tables together, it felt like a sign that I should put a book together with a story from each of us. I was going to be spending all day with these guys while we spoke to readers, and I thought that the option to grab a book with a story from each of us and get all 4 signatures inside would be a cool idea. I have been to several horror cons and as an avid reader and book collector, I always grab something from every writer at the convention. I have a load of signed books and I plan to get a whole lot more. I also thought it was pretty cool that we were all Scottish. There aren't a whole lot of Scottish Horror authors out there so the four of us ending up an a con together, even with it being in Scotland is still a pretty rare occurrence.

I took my idea to the authors in this book knowing that it would only work if the other three liked the idea and knowing I had very little time to pull the project together. About five weeks from pitching to being at the convention. You are holding the book so you know they all said yes. We used stories that we already had written. I went to my usual cover designer Michael Bray. As I write this foreword, we haven't done the cover yet, but I have given him my idea. I sent the four stories that we picked to my editor Ann Keeran, and we had the makings of a book.

I went back and forth on whether to keep it as a convention copy only book or to put it online and decided that I would like to get it into more people's hands. Stories are written to be read and I hope that you enjoy the ones inside this book.

I'd love to know what you guys think of this idea.

Whether you have grabbed a copy at the convention or picked it up on Kindle, I hope you love our stories.

Scottish Horror author, Kevin J. Kennedy.
Author of Halloween Land & The Clown.

Table of Contents

The Scaly Wages of Sin
By
Bill Davidson

Chocolate Covered Eyeball
By
John McNee

Crabs Vs the A.Y.T.
By
Kevin J. Kennedy

Those Damn Trees
By
David Sodergren

The Scaly Wages of Sin
By
Bill Davidson

Just before he got his nickel-plated Smith and Wesson and shot her in the chest, Greta told Phillip, "You know what you are? A walking, talking cliché."

They were alone on the yacht, Phillip having accidentally sacked all the staff, and had been meandering aimlessly around the Mediterranean hitting the booze hard on top of the blow and, in Phillip's case, acid.

Greta, wearing shapeless sweats and not so much as a trace of make-up, slumped on the cream leather of the wrap-around couch and did that thing that was really beginning to annoy him; lifting herself slightly before coming back down heavily, like making her point.

Phillip leaned forward to deliver a snappy come back, the sort of thing he was famous for, but all that came out of his mouth was, "So fuck?"

She raised an eyebrow. She was still beautiful, Greta, all that blonde hair and those lips, Jesus, that ass. But she'd stopped trying lately. Forgetting why she was here at all, in Phillips view. There was a definite slur to her voice when she asked, "That's all you've got? Really?"

"Yeah, so fuck."

He jabbed a thick thumb into his chest. "What you're forgetting, *every* bastard wants to be me. There's a reason somebody even gets to be a cliché."

"Everybody wants to be you? A chubby, greasy short ass with a shitty comb over. You think that big gold chain around your neck is cool? It's not cool. And lately it's damn near invisible in all that..."

She stuck out her chin and rolled her fingers around her throat.

"You've got a whole midriff where your neck should be."

Phillip just managed to avoid putting his hand up, or sucking his gut in. He lifted his glass, using it to point around the yacht. "Rich, is what I am. Only reason you're here."

Then, just a bit too late, the come-back occurred.

"*You're* the cliché. Ex-model. Married to an older guy she wouldn't be seen dead with, except for all of this."

"Yeah, well, just so you know, I'm done with it."

"Too true. You're letting yourself slip. Forgetting why you're here. Why I let you be here."

"So that I can put the Victoria's Secrets on, wiggle my ass to try to get some kinda rise outta your tired little pecker."

That was pretty much bang on the money, so he nodded. "What I hired you for."

"You didn't hire me, you moron. You married me. You revolt me, now we're finally being honest. So, sail this tub back to St Tropez or wherever, and let me off, you fat little asshole."

That was when Phillip stalked off to the bedroom, came back with the snub nosed 45. Greta raised a tired eyebrow. "This again? You're so full of shit Bergman, you think..."

The noise of the blast in the low-ceilinged room shocked Phillip, but not so much as the way the blood splattered out of her, a sudden spray side to side across the cream leather behind her back. Like a balloon bursting. But most shocking was the fact that he had actually pulled the trigger.

Her eyes were so very wide as she tried to speak, but words wouldn't come. You need functioning lungs for that, he thought, or at least a working tube between them and your mouth. She worked that mouth, up and down like a goldfish. Phillip shook the gun at her.

"You stupid, stupid, *stupid* bitch! All you had to do was look nice. Be sexy. That's it, nothing more."

She shook her head, lips trembling now, those huge blue eyes pleading. He took two steps forward and shot her again. Kept firing until something smacked him hard in his own chest.

He looked down at himself, horrified to see how blood splattered he was, his white cotton shirt sprayed red. He touched his breastbone and squealed with the pain of it. Jesus, a ricochet.

"No, no, no, no, no. Don't do this to me!"

He tore the buttons open, gasping in horror when he found something sticking out of him, right there in the middle of his chest. Not a bullet, he realised. A bit of bone. Her bone.

Dropping the gun, he ran to the bathroom and the mirror, waves of terror and revulsion going through him. Told himself not to flake out.

The bone fragment stuck out almost an inch. He went to touch it but couldn't bring himself to, not with his bare fingers, it was too disgusting, a bit of her bone actually *in* him. He dropped his head and closed his eyes, leaning heavily on the wash basin with both hands while he reached inside of himself for the strength and courage he knew was there.

Then he straightened and pointed at himself in the mirror.

"You got this Bergman. You know it."

Nodding at the right of it, he got a wad of tissue and used that to grip the disgusting fragment of his wife, having to pull hard to get it out. It came with a distinct snick that was too much too bear.

When Phillip came to, he found himself looking along the floor at the underside of the bath and there were cockroaches inches from his outstretched hand, three of the disgusting little bastards, feeding on blood that had splattered there.

They moved so fast, and one of them touched his thumb.

That got him moving, a horrified injection of adrenalin making him recoil, slithering his wide ass out of there. Worse, more of the little fuckers appeared, just as if they had been *underneath* him, skittering away like they thought he would try to stomp them. Fat chance of that.

All the money he had spent on pest control, and they just couldn't rid this boat of roaches. That was why the staff had gotten themselves sacked, couldn't they just keep the place clean? He hated bugs in general, they knew that, he told them over and over. He couldn't abide flies, but roaches. Roaches creeped him out the worst.

He wished he could take all those lazy bastards back on, so he could sack them again. See their faces.

On his feet now and breathing heavy, his legs feeling like they could barely hold him, he looked down at himself. He was so bloody, with that gash in his chest — an actual hole, look. He had to take a deep, restorative breath, because it was still bleeding.

He shook the thought of Greta, all the mess around her, out of his head. Deal with one thing at a time, that was the ticket. That's more the touch, as he would say back in his market trader days.

Try to take on that horror too soon... oh no. No thank you, my friend. That way lies madness.

Searider III, big, white and beautiful, rode the waves easily, somewhere close to the middle of the Med. Almost certainly.

Phillip stripped all his clothes off and got into the shower, spending a good twenty minutes soaping and shampooing himself. The hole in his chest stung, but at least it was clean.

Once he had applied some gauze, changed, did a couple of lines and refreshed his whisky, he felt so much better. His bloodied clothes went straight into the sea, no point thinking any harder about it than that.

Greta was in a smallish room at the bow of the ship, the one she used to like to call the snug. Just another irritating thing she did. God, that woman.

She was infuriating. Calling rooms on yachts snugs and doing all that yoga and shit, like she was rubbing his nose in it. Pretending she wanted him to do it with her.

It occurred to Phillip that he could just close the door and leave her there. The fuel tanks were almost full, the kitchen was stocked, no reason to go near land for weeks.

But, he had to go look.

Jesus, the mess of her. He couldn't resist giving a long, low whistle and shaking his head at the impressive extent of the damage. Being careful not to step in any of the blood, he walked one way and then the other, just taking it in.

"I gave you fair warning, girlie. Can't say I didn't. You should've thought better. Don't poke the fuckin' bear!"

He almost slapped his chest as he said this, but the ache in his chest stopped him, just in time.

He sipped his whisky, considering the problem, how to clean this up. As he stood there, stalled for the moment, a fly buzzed past his head, making him jump before it landed on her. A blowfly, this one. Fat and hairy and lazy.

"Jesus. Where did you come from?"

He gave himself a shake and took a healthy gulp of Glenmorangie, thought then about dragging her to the side and tipping her straight into the water. Fetching towels and cleaning fluid.

It was, Phillip eventually decided, simply too much for a person to deal with right now. Only hours ago, she had still been bitching at him, making fun of his neck and making him fucking shoot her. He was probably quite badly traumatized. Needed a day or so to regain his equilibrium before getting to grips with her Godawful mess.

Phillip lost the plot for a while, a good while. He was man enough to admit that to himself. He dropped a tab of acid and hit the blow and the booze hard. Also, that skunk was too damn strong for anybody's mental health, especially when you've got the body of your decomposing wife in the mix.

On deck one bright, sparkling morning he threw his arms wide.

"Jesus", he shouted, yelling it across the wide, empty sea.

"A little consideration here, *please*. These aren't normal fucking circumstances, you know. Not normal at all."

The wound on his chest kept scabbing over and breaking open again. It throbbed, and he suspected he might end up with a scar. Maybe, and this was a horrible thought, maybe even a dent.

Still, everything might have been manageable if she had only been decomposing. If all he had to put up with was some pain in his chest and a bit of stink, he was sure he would have got his ass in there and gone to *work*. He was a man who took care of business, everybody knew that, and that reeking bitch would be gone. The place would be sparkling clean.

If she had only been decomposing.

He felt another wave of anger at those lazy bastards, the ones who he'd paid good money to keep the yacht free from insects.

That one fly, Jesus. He had read that flies can get through their life cycle in a couple of days in warm weather and it was hot as hell on the water. One fly lays who knows how many eggs. Thousands probably. They hatch and in a couple of days there are thousands of thousands. In other words, millions.

The last time he had steeled himself to go into the snug, he'd been frozen to the spot. Had to shake himself like a dog and take a deep gulp of whisky just to start breathing again.

Because she had moved. He ought to have turned himself around, got out of there before this sight got too deeply seared into his brain, but he was stuck. Feet glued to the floor, jaw hanging open, hand still on the door handle.

He had noticed the background drone for days, but didn't admit to himself what it was until he opened that door and found the air sickeningly full of obese blow-flies. So fat and hairy it was a wonder they could get off the ground. The door had pushed a drift of their dried carcasses across the floor as he entered, and more were piled six inches high against the windows.

The stink and the noise and the movement, all those flies, lazy in the air.

And their younger selves, huge white maggots, nothing lazy about them as they swam around in their own gluey liquor. Every inch of Greta was in constant movement, those worms slithering and slinking around and around.

And not just flies. It might have been okay if it was just blow-flies. Greta fairly teemed with cockroaches, skittering over her like she was gravy. As he watched, his whisky breath stuttering in his throat, her head slipped to the side so that what was left of her face was pointed his way, like she had turned to look at him.

All her flesh was being consumed but those amazing, beautiful eyes that had caught him for the first time across a room full of bankers and city boys were still there. They were, if anything, bigger now, and just as blue.

What got him out of there was a particularly large and clumsy blow-fly hitting the side of his head. He took a stiff and shaky step backwards, and pulled the door closed amid a swarm of escapees. Turned the latch, because he had no intention of going back in there.

Fuck that for a game of soldiers.

Nights became the worst. During the day his music blared over the speakers and he sailed Searider around, turning from any other craft that appeared on the horizon, but at night he could hear the drone of the flies and the skitter of the cockroaches. He stopped putting the lights off altogether, because that's when the little fuckers came out.

One night, he lay sweating, unable to sleep despite the booze and the tablets. But it seemed he must have flaked out because he came awake to the sound of his own snore and the memory of a deep thud. The memory was in his bones, like somebody damned heavy had just jumped aboard the yacht.

He reached for his revolver, but it wasn't there. It was on the floor in the snug. Picking up a bottle by the neck, he crept to the door, opened it a crack and listened. Nothing. Trying to get a handle on his breathing, he crept across the main living area. He could hear the incessant drone coming from the snug, skitterings everywhere. This boat was alive with insects now, the sort you did *not* want to step onto.

He hurried on deck, a naked, drunk man holding a bottle by the neck, and checked the water each side, wondering if he might see another boat or a dinghy moored up to the yacht. Still nothing.

The next thud, when it came, came from the door to the snug. Standing six feet away, Phillip took an involuntary step back, then shook his head. This was the sound of something heavy hitting the door, nothing an insect could make. Heavy and...he didn't want to think the next word, but it came to him anyway. Heavy and wet.

He actually saw the next blow, its impact on the thin wood, the door warping for a second in its frame. Phillip danced on the spot, the bottle useless in his hand. Looked around as if he could find an explanation. A clue to what was happening.

"I wish I was wearing socks."

The next blow caused the wood to crack and splinter and he turned and scurried away. Just as if there was some place to go.

When the door to his bedroom opened, Phillip was in bed, knees high with his sheets pulled up to his nose.

Greta sidled in and stood in the doorway, in a pose he knew well. One arm up and against the frame, the other on her exaggeratedly cocked hip. He used to think of it as her *here it comes big boy*, pose.

But that was in the days when she came with skin. Now, she was made of maggots and roaches, thousands of them boiling across her, coming to the surface before diving beneath tunnels of bone. Massive blow-flies flew above, spinning around her still golden hair, like a halo.

Her eyeballs, for reasons known only to flies, remained untouched. She looked at him from out of all that blue and maggots receded from teeth and jaw in a grotesque imitation of a smile. A cockroach eyebrow raised in that familiar expression.

That was when Phillip screamed for the first time. And it was the first time she laughed, the sound coming, not from her mouth, but the gaping hole in her chest, where a bullet had blasted the sternum from the ribs. At least it had the rhythm of a laugh, one made by rubbing cockroaches together.

It didn't seem likely that he could speak, and there was a lot of stuttering and teeth chattering, but eventually he managed to say, "Please. Please, Greta. It's me, Phillip. If you still have any love for me, leave me be."

In response, she pushed herself away from the door frame and sashayed into the room. Greta always had a sexy, fleshy sashay. Maggots and roaches dripped from her as she moved to the end of the bed and turned her back to look over her shoulder at him, winked and bent deeply from the waist, sliding her hand down her leg.

"Isn't this what you like? The way you like it?"

Her voice was hellish, but he could understand every word. She straightened, as if something had just occurred to her. "Wait, now. Hold your horses, big fella."

He did wait, thinking that his heart, which was hammering high and crazy in his throat, would surely burst. In that moment, he prayed it would.

"Wait. I'm not ready for you yet, you bad, bad boy."

Some of the insects that were dropping from her were scurrying or writhing across the bedspread and he squeaked and tried to shake them off as she walked, taking her own sweet time, to her dressing table. What passed for skin still seethed as she sat and picked up a lipstick.

He could see in the mirror as she rolled it out, his favourite deep red, of course it was.

Greta puckered up, and slowly applied the lipstick, smearing maggots waxy red. When she turned to smile again, head to one side in that way she always did, he screamed for the second time.

Phillip had always enjoyed watching her put sexy clothes on for him, stockings, garter belt and high heels. He watched her do that now, thinking about the gun lying in the other room, and whether it might have a bullet left in it. One would be enough.

Finally, wearing her best lingerie, the insects around her mouth still slathered in red, she came for him. When she crawled onto the bed, he screamed and screamed so his eyes and head might burst and would not stop.

"Phillip! Phillip what is it?"

Phillip opened his eyes, and it wasn't night. It was day. He could feel the ache in his head and the sourness inside and when he licked his lips they were dried and chapped. Moving tentatively, he touched his chest but there was no wound. He forced himself to turn to look and there was Greta, tanned and whole and so beautiful it took his breath away, just like that first time, in a room full of bankers. Her blonde hair tumbled over her shoulders.

Her eyes were a thousand miles of purest blue.

Still, he jerked away from her, pulling the bedclothes around himself as he slithered back as far as he could. She blinked, and pulled her hands to her chest, looking hurt.

It was a long moment before she said, "You got to stop taking all that shit, honey. I'm worried about you. I mean really."

He sat up and stared at her, stared at himself, opened his hands and looked at them. Seconds ticked by and they stayed like that, the two of them. Finally, she came onto the bed and reached out slowly, to put a hand on his arm. He watched it coming, horrified.

But it was just a hand.

She leaned closer. "You're really scaring me this time."

His throat hurt, badly like something in there was torn, and his voice, when he spoke, sounded hoarse and strained. "Are you okay?"

She shrugged, sheepish suddenly. "A bit hungover. Rough around the edges, but I've kept away from the hard stuff. But you. You got to get yourself straight. I mean it this time."

He nodded. "I dropped acid. A lot of it."

"No shit. You've been on a week-long trip, I don't know where you've been. Jesus. You were screaming your lungs out last night. Time to stop, okay?"

He put his head in his hands and wept then, and she hugged him to her chest, crooning softly. After a while, having his face pushed against those fantastic breasts began to have the usual effect, and she noticed.

Greta kissed him deeply, a long, long kiss. Then she pulled off her shirt and hauled the covers back, coming astride him.

"Greta…"

"Shhhh. It's okay, you bad, bad, boy."

She was touching him, her clever fingers bringing him fully erect, and he wanted her, maybe more than ever before. He reached for her but she slapped his hands away, harder than was necessary, he thought. Hard enough to hurt.

She leaned in to whisper. "Hold your horses. You *gunslinger*."

He gasped as she lowered herself onto him and closed his eyes as she started to move.

He kept his eyes closed as he slid his hands over her, her skin so smooth and slick, like wet silk. Why should she be so wet?

He jerked at a sudden sharp hitching feeling in his chest and cracked his lids to see a fat cockroach wriggle out of the gash in his sternum. He stared hard at himself, not wanting to look up, but eventually had to raise his head.

To see what was above him.

The End

Chocolate Covered Eyeball
By
John McNee

The kid with his arm elbow-deep in a barrel of watermelon taffy wore an outfit of grey and blue rags. Scraps of what looked like old carpet hung from his waist and tufts of frayed cloth had been stapled to his chest. The whole ratty ensemble had been finished with a sea captain's hat planted firmly atop his greasy head.

"So what are you supposed to be?" Cam asked.

The kid, who looked to be in his late teens, turned slowly around to fix Cam with the kind of expression that suggested he was too high to know who or where he was with any degree of certainty. "Huh?"

"The costume," Cam said. "Who are you?"

"Huh?" the kid repeated, then glanced down to get a look at himself. "Oh yeah." He brightened suddenly and grinned. "I'm Navel Lint. Get it?"

Cam did, but almost wished he didn't. "Very clever," he said. "You know, in my day, when we dressed up, we actually dressed up as something scary. Vampires, demons, zombies. Y'know... Halloween stuff?"

The kid's grin morphed into a pained expression that implied Cam was using way too many words way too quickly. "Screw off," he said, fished a handful of taffy from the barrel, dropped it into his sack and shuffled away.

Cam, staying right where he was, called after him, "Y'know in my day, we didn't say things like 'screw off' either. We said 'fu...'"

"Cam!" Becca called to him from the other side of the

store. He looked and saw her manoeuvring through the crowd of cosplay characters, 'sexy' spooks and personified puns, easily identifiable by her non-costume of t-shirt, shorts and sandals. She had a big grin on her face and was holding up a clear plastic bag filled with dark brown candy. "Look! They have Chicos!"

"What are Chicos?"

"Chocolate flavoured jelly babies," she said, holding the bag out so he could get a closer look. "They're practically impossible to find outside of Australia because some people think they're racist, which obviously is bullshit."

"No kidding. They'll be the old man's own version, you know. He doesn't sell brands."

"Well they look just like the real thing," she said, then put the bag to her nose and inhaled deeply. "And they smell exactly right! Y'know, I can't believe this place is closing. It's such a shame!"

"Sure it is." Cam said, and moved away from the taffy barrels, making way for the line that had formed behind him.

Becca followed as he made his way to the end of the aisle, stopping at a display with dozens of orange, pumpkin-shaped jars arranged in a pyramid. "Are you upset?" she asked.

"What?"

"You don't seem in a good mood. Is it because the store's closing down? I know it's sad. You're losing a piece of your childhood."

He scoffed. "I could give a shit what happens to Koolter's Candy."

"Shh! He'll hear you!" Becca's pony-tail danced as she swung her head in the direction of the counter and the elderly bald man who stood behind it. He didn't look back. Returning her attention to Cam she said, "I thought you said you were in here all the time as a kid?"

"We were. Me and my buddy Nicky used to come here every other day. But it wasn't to buy. And it sure wasn't because we liked Old Man Koolter."

"Then what?"

He gave her a look that said she was slow to catch on. "To steal. Obviously."

Sharp intake of breath. "Oh I don't approve of that."

"We were here all the time. All the damn time." Cam stared down the aisle, looking for a moment like he was watching himself, some twenty-odd years in the past. "It was the most fun I ever had."

"Didn't he ever catch you?"

"Only once." Cam's smile faded as he recalled the memory. "I haven't been back since."

Becca stared down at the bag in her hand and shook her head. "I feel so used. I've been indulging the wrong kind of nostalgia. Led here under false pretences!" She poked him hard with her elbow.

Cam laughed, nudged her back and pointed at one of the jars. "Have you seen these?"

She looked where he was pointing and read the label: 'LICORICE LARVAE'.

"Eww," she said and wrinkled her nose, then read the other jars. 'SOUR BATS' read one. 'JELLIED BRAINS', 'OOZING BLOOD BON BONS', 'GUMMY TONGUES' and 'SUGAR RAZOR BLADES' were among the others.

"Anything take your interest?"

She shrugged. "I'm sure I'd have loved them all when I was nine." She pointed to the jar at the top of the pyramid and read out the label. "Chocolate covered eyeballs. Now that is pretty gross."

Cam grinned. "Those are his real speciality. It's what he was most famous for. People used to come from all across the county to shop here at Halloween. From all across the state. All to pick up some glorified gummy worms and a bag of chocolate covered eyeballs."

"It's very creative. And gross. Gross and creative." She took another look around the store, at the assortment of baskets, jars, tins and barrels overflowing with candy, and the costumed customers shuffling down the aisles. "He's still got an awful lot of stock left for someone who's going out of business."

"That doesn't surprise me."

"Probably helps that no-one's trying to rob him blind," she said, eyeing him with blatant distaste. When he didn't rise to the bait she said, "I suppose Halloween must be boom time for the confectioners. This'll probably be his last, big payday before it's all over. One final, bittersweet hurrah."

"Oh, it's a real tragedy," said Cam, sounding like he couldn't possibly mean it less. "You about done?"

"Yeah, I've just got to pay for the Chicos. Get you outside?"

He nodded and she left him, weaving her way back through the crowd to reach the counter.

Old Man Koolter – which Becca now couldn't help calling him, having heard Cam use the name so many times – was leaning over a yellow-paged ledger, using a fountain pen to mark down the latest sale. She watched as his fingers dragged the pen ever so slowly across the page, waiting patiently till he was finished. When he did, he placed down the pen, lifted his head and fixed her with a quizzical look, as though confused as to why she was there.

"Hi," she said and held out her bag.

The smile that crept up his face moved about as quickly as his handwriting. He said nothing, but took the bag from her, moved to the end of the counter and dropped it into a set of brass scales.

"You have a lovely shop," Becca said.

"Thank you." His voice was a rasp, barely rising above a whisper.

"When do you actually close?"

"Not for a few weeks yet, I should say. Depends how long I can make the stocks last."

"I was just saying how it's such a shame. I'd have been in here every day."

"Why haven't you?" Koolter asked, without taking his eyes off the scale. There was no obvious malice in the question. Irritability, sure, but not malice.

"Oh, we only just moved here," she said. "Just a couple of nights ago, actually, into, um… Thorp Street? This is my first visit into town, so… It's my boyfriend's place. My boyfriend's parents' place. We're renovating." She knew she was probably telling more than he wanted to hear, but felt the need to explain herself. Didn't want him thinking she was someone who had lived in the town for years, ignoring the candy store while it struggled.

"Well now." This time the old man's smile had something like a little warmth in it, showing a flash of teeth that were too white to be real. "And from where do you hail?"

"Australia. Well… Boston, more recently, but New South Wales before that."

"How special. And what do you make of Hollybrook?"

"Oh it's lovely, just lovely. And all the trees, especially in autumn. The leaves… It's really beautiful."

"Thorp Street..." Koolter muttered to himself as he cut a strip of orange ribbon from a roll on his left, pinched the bag of Chicos and tied a bow around it. "Thorp Street. Joe and Nora Ratliff just moved out of Thorp Street."

"Yes!" Becca gasped and grinned. "The Ratliffs! That's them! They've moved down to Florida so we've moved into the house to fix it up and flip it."

Koolter nodded, satisfied. "Knew them well. I guess that means you'll be courting young Campbell Ratliff."

Her jaw dropped. "You know Cam?"

He nodded. "Oh yes."

She leaned on the counter and squinted at him, cheekily. "Do you know everyone, Mr Koolter?"

"Most people. But then I've been here a very long time."

"I bet you know this town like the back of your hand."

"Indeed." He held the bag out towards her and her eyes went to his hand, seeing the symbol drawn on the skin just below the knuckle. Eight black arrows pointing from a centre circle. It looked like a tattoo, but could have been drawn in eyeliner pencil for all she could tell.

"Is that for Halloween?" she asked.

Old Man Koolter looked where she looked and chuckled, sheepishly, as though he'd forgotten the mark was there. Slowly, his fingers curled to form devil horns and he raised them above his head. "Hail Satan."

She laughed, internally noting the moment as the cutest thing she'd seen all day. She took the bag and opened her purse. "Thanks a lot. What do I owe you?"

He shook his head. "It's yours. With my compliments. Welcome to the neighbourhood."

***

"He was so nice," Becca declared, as they strolled back through town. "I almost cried when he wouldn't let me pay. It was just so sweet!"

"I'm sure," said Cam.

"How old do you think he is?"

"I don't know. A thousand? Old Man Koolter was ancient when I was a kid. And he hasn't gotten any younger since then."

They took a different route through the neighbourhood than the way they'd come, passing family homes bedecked in all the sinister paraphernalia of the season. Front lawns had been converted into cemeteries with the erection of plywood gravestones. Glowing pumpkins lined the driveways. Giant cobwebs clung to the walls and windows.

"This is amazing. It's like being in a film," Becca said, autumn leaves circling her in ankle-high whirlwinds.

"Oh come on. I'm sure you had plenty of Halloweens just like this back home."

"Nope."

"No?"

"Australians don't celebrate Halloween."

"You don't?"

"No. Well yeah, I mean... some people do. The same way some people will celebrate anything American, but it's not a national thing or even that big of a deal. There are costume parties and parades, mostly in the cities, but no trick or treating or anything."

"I didn't know that."

"You shouldn't assume your childhood experiences are universal, Cam. We didn't all have Halloween and we weren't all sticky-fingered juvenile delinquents."

"I know that. I just…" Cam had his eyes on the ground ahead of him. "Seems like a shame. Trick or treating was always the best part. You missed out."

"It wouldn't have mattered where I grew up. Hard to go door-to-door when the nearest neighbour lives five miles away. Halloween's one of those holidays that doesn't really work outside of the suburbs. You can't presume it's the same for everyone."

"I didn't. I don't. Even here it's not the same. What happens in Hollybrook is different from what happens in Allanstown is different from what happens in Norwood."

"I don't know any of those places."

"Sorry." He laughed. "Next towns over."

"And they don't celebrate Halloween?"

"They do, but… it's different. What one neighbourhood does can be different, even. Take here. Now you'd probably guess that kids, when they go out tonight, will have to knock on doors to get candy, but they won't."

"No?"

"No, round here you leave candy out on the stoop, porch or top step and let the kids come and grab a handful themselves. You just leave them to it. The grown-ups don't even supervise."

"Oh wow," Becca rolled her eyes. "What a tremendous difference, Cam. I'm so amazed."

"I'm just saying it's not the same as other places, that's all. And I don't know when it happened, when everybody got together and decided that was how they were going to do it. My Dad said when he was a kid he still had to knock on doors and take what was given. And my granddad said in his day, when kids went to doors, they had to sing a song or tell a joke or in some way perform some kind of trick to earn their... I dunno, aniseed balls or bazooka joes or whatever kind of lousy excuse for a candy they had back then."

"And now kids today can just help themselves to as much as they want."

"Right."

"And you don't approve."

"I don't. It's bad enough that we just pile it up on our doorsteps so kids can come and grab as much as they like, but you know what's worse? They don't. They grab their favourites and move on to the pile at the next house. And they can do that because there's nothing special about candy to them. They eat candy every day. It's everywhere. As much as they want all the time."

"I'm not sure how many children would agree with you."

"Because they don't even know how lucky they are. When I was their age candy was all I could think about."

She laughed. "A criminal obsession."

"I'm not kidding. You have no idea the kind of things my friends and I would do, the shit we would pull, just to get our hands on a little candy."

"I've got some idea," she said, referencing his confession of his criminal past back at the candy store.

"I don't just mean Koolter's. It was my entire childhood. And Halloween was the biggest day of the year. Forget the costumes and the scary movies and the rest... it was the candy! That's what made it so incredible. Now it's just like any other day."

She put a hand on his shoulder. "Cam, I'm sorry. I had no idea you were wallowing in such nostalgic grief."

"You think it's funny."

"No," she said, trying to force her face not to smile. "Not if you don't."

"I know it sounds frivolous. But I liked being a kid, up to a point. I liked growing up here. And it seems that everything that made it special is being all worn away."

"The world changes. Nothing stays the same. That's what growing up's all about."

He sighed. "I bet I sound like a grumpy old man."

"Just a little. I'm sure Mr Koolter would agree with you. It's probably what's led to the closure of his business."

Cam chuckled and took something from the inside pocket of his coat. "Then there's always a bright side."

"What's that?" Becca asked, pointing to the bag in his hand.

"Oh, this?" He produced a small brown globe and popped it in his mouth. "Want one?"

He held the bag out to her and she peered inside. "Chocolate covered eyeballs?"

He nodded, his cheek swollen from the item lodged in it.

Intrigued, she took one out and raised it up, studying its smoothly polished surface. "What's on the inside?"

"Guess," Cam said, now chewing.

Becca looked back at him, then at the bag. "When did you buy those?"

Cam shrugged.

"I was at the counter when you went outside. You never brought anything up. I didn't see you pay for anything."

He took another treat from the bag and bit into it. "Crime never tasted so sweet."

"You stole it?" She cried, genuinely appalled.

"Couldn't help it." He shrugged again. "It was just there for the taking."

"You shoplifted chocolate from a harmless old man?"

"Oh relax, he's not so harmless."

"He's about a hundred years old! And you're supposed to be thirty-four, not twelve!"

"What does it matter? This time next week he won't even have a candy store. He's not going to miss a little bag of chocolate."

"He's an old man!"

"It's the least he deserves."

"Why do you keep saying things like that? Ever since we went in that store you've been making weird little comments like that."

"It doesn't matter."

"You're just being mean for the sake of it?"

"Listen, I could tell you a couple of stories about Koolter that might make you realize he's not so wonderful, okay?"

"Oh really? What is he? A Nazi war criminal?"

Cam laughed, mirthlessly. "I wouldn't be surprised."

She stopped walking. "Tell me. Seriously. I'd like to know."

Cam looked at her for a moment, then at the piece of candy in her hand. "It's melting," he said.

She looked and saw the chocolate dribbling down her fingers. As much as it felt, in some small way, like collusion, she popped it into her mouth then licked her fingers clean. "Peanut-butter," she said, chewing.

"You were expecting something else?"

"I'm a little disappointed," she admitted. "Now tell me."

He started walking again. "I'll tell you why I never felt bad about stealing from him. That's because he steals. I heard rumours about him from other kids when I was growing up. They said he'd pick pockets, burgle houses, even mug children. Never for money, just for candy."

"Oh come on, Cam. This is a bad start if you want me on your side."

"You know the way kids talk," he said. "They talked about Old Man Koolter like he was a bald demon who literally stole candy from babies. And because I was a kid too I accepted what they said, but I didn't really believe it... until I saw it for myself."

Becca didn't buy a word, but she was enjoying the story. "Give me another one of those," she said, motioning to the bag in his hand.

Cam handed it over to her. "I was ten years old and it was Halloween. The trick or treating was all done, I'd taken my costume off and I was in my room, counting my candy. It was midnight."

"I have an image in my head of you sitting on a pile the size of Kilimanjaro."

"It wasn't that big. I was a little annoyed with myself for not taking more when I had the chance. And then I had this great idea. All the trick-or-treaters had gone home. But I knew that a lot of candy would still be sitting out on people's porches, unclaimed, and would stay there till the morning."

"So you realized you could sneak out while the rest of the world was asleep and claim all the leftovers for yourself."

"I did."

"Sneaky sneaky," she said, speaking around a mouthful of chocolate.

"But then I went to the window... and saw Old Man Koolter had already beaten me to it."

Becca's eyes widened. "Seriously?"

Cam nodded slowly. "He was creeping from one house to

the next, dragging a big sack behind him like some kind of emaciated reverse-Santa Claus. And I watched as he scooped up everything he could find and dumped it inside."

"How long did you watch him for?"

"Till he was out of sight. But he swept those steps clean. Not so much as an empty wrapper left in his wake."

"Did he see you?"

Cam was silent for a moment, considering the question. "No. There was a moment where I thought he did. I thought he looked round and smiled, but… no. It wouldn't have been possible."

"But… why? Why would he do something like that?"

"My guess? So he could repack and resell it. Scavenge what he could, break it all apart, melt it down and mould it into something else. Something with the look of an artisan that he could tie a bow around and sell at double the market price. That's pure profit for a man willing to put in the effort. What was it you called Halloween? Boom time? I'm betting it was a nice little bonus for him."

Becca looked at the bag of chocolate and peanut-butter balls in her hand. "That's crazy."

"What can I tell you? It happened. And I never felt guilty about stealing candy from him because I knew it didn't cost him anything to make it."

They arrived at Thorp Street. "What else?"

"Hmm?"

"You said you could tell me a couple of stories. What else?"

"Oh, it doesn't matter…"

"Stop telling me that and just tell me. What? Was he stealing honey from bees? Does he have a gingerbread house I should know about?"

It was clear she was trying to make him laugh, but he didn't. "I'm pretty sure he murdered my best friend."

That changed the mood. "What?" Becca asked, hoping she'd misheard.

"My friend Nicky. My best friend. Pretty much my only friend back then, actually. We weren't well liked by other kids. We did a lot of stupid things. Pranks. The usual bratty stuff, like shoplifting from Koolter's. Nicky taught me how to do it without anyone noticing. But then there was the day the old man finally did notice."

Becca didn't say anything for a few seconds, not sure she wanted to probe any more. But finally her lips moved. "What did he do?"

Cam stared up into the trees over their heads, eyes narrowed like he was trying to read their branches. "He... cursed us."

"He what?"

"I was scared out of my mind," Cam said. "He locked the door and we were trapped in there with him. I was too terrified to remember everything he said word for word, but it was like he tried to put some kind of spell on us. He said there was nothing more disgusting in the world than a thief, if you can believe that. And he warned that if we ever stole from him again there'd be no way to hide it. Whatever we took, he would get back. With interest."

"What the hell does that mean?"

"I don't know. I just wanted out of there. When he unlocked the door I was so relieved I ran all the way home."

"It sounds like he was just trying to scare you, Cam."

"It does sound like that. And it worked, at least on me. But

Nicky wasn't scared. I knew he'd go back. I knew he'd try again. And a few weeks later he was gone."

"Gone?"

"Just disappeared one night, right out of his own room. Had dinner, had a bath, went to bed. By morning he'd vanished without a trace."

"That's terrible."

"When the cops searched his room they couldn't find any evidence that anyone had broken in, no signs of a struggle, no blood. But they found a lot of Koolter's candy. More than a kid like Nicky could afford."

"What happened then?"

Cam took a deep breath before continuing. "I'd like to say it tore the town apart, but that wouldn't be true. I remember there was an investigation, but... it seemed to be over real fast. No evidence, no suspects. I tried telling my parents about Old Man Koolter, but they didn't believe me. They made me feel so stupid and ridiculous that when a detective came to ask me questions I didn't even mention it to him. He was in and gone in five minutes. And everybody just got on with their lives. Like I said, kids like me and Nicky weren't especially well liked. Most people didn't notice he was gone. I would still see his parents around town for years afterwards, but I never spoke to them. It wasn't even that long before I moved on. It was like he'd just moved to a different town or school. No big deal. Nothing to cry about. But I never went back in that damn store. Not till today."

Cam stopped walking and looked over Becca's shoulder. She turned and saw that they had arrived back at the house. She looked again at Cam, brow furrowed, said nothing, then stepped through the gate, walked up the path to the porch and sat down.

He stayed out on the sidewalk for a few moments, letting her have some time with her own thoughts, then joined her. "Well?"

"Well what?" she said, staring out at the street.

"What do you think?"

"I think it's a horrible story and I wish you hadn't had to go through anything like that."

"But?"

She sighed. "But... child abductions happen. They happen all over the world. And the cause, to my knowledge, has never been a Halloween candy vendetta."

"You think I'm wrong?"

"I think..." She rubbed her hand across her forehead, as though trying to stimulate her mind into forming a coherent argument. "I think you were ten years old when this happened. I think you had a very limited point of view. You were denied the kind of perspective that your parents, or Nicky's parents or the police had. I think two incidents of very great importance to you happened in close proximity to one another and you married them up because... because they were all you had." She reached out to him and grasped his hand. "I think you blamed yourself for not telling the police about Koolter and you've been carrying that guilt around with you for a long time. I think guilt, more than anything else, is what makes you think he's responsible. It's a powerful emotion that way. But what happened to your friend, Cam? It's not your fault. And it's not Mr Koolter's fault."

Cam had been nodding the whole way through her speech. He kept nodding after she finished, eyes on the overgrown lawn before them.

She squeezed his hand. "I'm not saying that I don't believe you, Cam. Just..."

"I know what you're saying," he said. "And you're right. I know you're right. It's just... it's a hard thing to let go of." He stood. "And whatever else, I'll never feel bad about stealing from that son of a bitch." He fished the house keys from his pocket and stepped up to the door.

Becca stood, instinctively brushed down her shorts and surveyed the dilapidated porch. "We should have bought some candy to leave out. Y'know, just in case anybody comes by."

"Yeah probably," Cam said, unlocked the door and stepped inside.

Becca looked again at the scrunched-up bag in her hand. There were around half a dozen eyeballs left. She set it down on the top step then followed after him.

***

Cam knew he was going to puke even before he woke up. His dreams told him as much. A furious cavalcade of lurid colors and grotesque melting faces devoid of characters or narrative, they served as an unconscious mirror to the violent churning of acids and half-digested foodstuff in his gut. He opened his eyes to find his feet already out of the bed and halfway to the floor, moving before he'd had a chance to make up his mind. He put a hand to his stomach, feeling the vibrations as the forces within rebelled against him, their whines and groans loud in his ear.

With a whine of his own he pitched himself forward, out of the bed, and stumbled into the bathroom, throwing out a hand to the wall and slapping on the light.

"Cam?" Becca, with her back to him, stirred briefly, but didn't rise.

He was hardly in a position to answer, already crouching down towards the toilet bowl, an icy shiver through his limbs – a tremor before the eruption. He coughed.

Oh God. Here it comes.

His eyes were closed during the torrent, but he felt and heard the force of it as it hit with the power of a water cannon. Rounds two and three followed before he had a chance to even inhale, sending up spray across his forehead and chin.

And then it stopped.

Sticky strands dangling from his lips, a taste of sugar on his tongue, he opened his bloodshot eyes to behold a scene from a surrealist painter's wet dream.

There was a kaleidoscope on his toilet. A whirl of vibrant colours – fluorescent pinks and greens, yellows and reds. A vortex of liquid neon, frothing like ice-cream in soda. And bobbing in the midst of the toxic technicolour soup were pieces of candy – jelly beans and Junior mints, gummy bears and gobstoppers, peach rings and peppermint patties. More than he'd eaten that day. Things he hadn't eaten in years. Things he'd never tasted in his life.

He blinked, but the mess didn't disappear. It sat there and steeped. Horrified, he put a hand to his face, ran it through his hair – and pulled half of it out at the roots.

Bringing his hand down to his face, he saw it wasn't hair he clutched, but a tangle of black liquorice laces.

He struggled up onto his feet – legs reluctant to comply with his commands, turned to the mirror, and screamed.

The sound was enough to shock Becca from her slumber. She threw out her limbs like a startled cat, scattering bed-sheets and landing in a kneeling position on the bed. "Cam! Cam, what's wrong?" She looked towards the bathroom as her boyfriend stumbled into view, then threw her hands up to her face and gasped.

The figure in the doorway did not look like Cam. It wore his t-shirt and boxers. When it moaned, it sounded like him. But in other respects, it barely even appeared human. Liquorice hair clung to marzipan skin, dappled by syrup-like sweat. Waxy red lips parted to reveal a tongue of flapping red gelatin. When he tried to speak, teeth tumbled from his mouth, clattering on the floor like mints.

Becca was frozen, unable to process what she was seeing.

He staggered towards her and threw up a hand. Sugar crystals glittered in the skin of his fingers as they grasped for her.

Shrieking, she tried to slap it away. The blow snapped the fingers from his hand and sent them spinning into a corner of the room. A glance at the stumps revealed an interior of honeycomb, oozing malic acid like blood.

She screamed again and he ran, tearing out of the room like a monster, weaving from side to side, colliding with furniture and fittings as he tried to navigate his way downstairs on legs of sorbitol and modified corn starch, cocoa butter and soya lecithin, carnauba wax and powdered whey protein.

What remained of his honeycomb hands began to shatter as he wrapped them around the handle to the front door and threw it wide. He tried to scream for help, but struggled to get air into his caramel lungs or manipulate his fondant vocal chords.

His vision was failing him as he crossed the porch. Tripping over something on the top step his peanut brittle bones snapped and he went down. He hit the dirt on his back and felt his limbs shatter, pieces rolling away from each other, disassembling beneath a cloud of sherbet and reforming into new shapes, flavours and crispy coated shells.

"Cam!" He could hear Becca calling from inside the house, just audible through the wall of cotton candy in his ears. Only slightly louder was the sound of the gate swinging open.

His head lolled round like a giant lollipop free of its stick. As the syrup crystalised in his veins and his marshmallow heart seized, in the instant before he went blind, he saw a figure approach.

"Cam, I'm calling an ambu…!" Becca's words died on her tongue as she reached the porch and saw what was left of her boyfriend.

She froze, phone in hand raised high, and stared at the scattered mess of confectionery spilling out of his clothes, the central pile only vaguely resembling a human form.

Old Man Koolter was standing over him, his bald head gleaming in the moonlight, the end of a cloth sack clutched in his hand. Looking to Becca, he grinned, lifted his other hand, and waved.

She dropped into a crouching position, letting the phone fall. "What did you do?"

Koolter pointed below her, to the small bag she'd left on the porch step, still half full. "He did it to himself. I warned him a long time ago what would happen."

Becca felt sick. She could feel her stomach doing cartwheels, threatening to empty its contents on the lawn. Eyes darting between the bag at her feet and Cam, she wondered if she was about to suffer the same fate. "I ate it," she said. "I ate it too."

Koolter's grin stretched a little wider. "It's yours. With my compliments."

Then he bowed, stretched a hand down to what remained of Cam's face and plucked from it a single sphere of candy-coated confection.

The End

Crabs Vs the A.Y.T.
By
Kevin J. Kennedy

Cataclysmic storms had ravished the UK. It was a small island to begin with, but the recent torrent of tsunamis had destroyed its shores and wrecked everything for miles inland in every direction. National services worked around the clock to save survivors. The news updated the rising death toll every few hours. Whole families had been lost, entire farms washed away, buildings destroyed, and large sections of land flooded and blocked off from everywhere else.

Another problem was the sea life that were left behind. The giant waves had brought with them all manner of sea creatures, and as the waters receded, they remained. Most were dead: seals, dolphins, whales, sharks, countless fish, and jellyfish but most of all — crabs. The crabs were one of the few creatures that had survived. Everywhere you looked, you could see them scuttling. At first, they stuck to the shadows, dashing under cars and into hedges. As the days passed by and people were focused on rescuing their own kind and salvaging food and supplies, the crabs gathered. No one noticed until it was too late. That is when the next stage of destruction began.

"Mate, pass me that bucket kit over," wee Tommy said.

"Get up n' get it yourself, ya lazy wee dick," Zanda replied.

"Fuck sake, man. Lazy cunt," Tommy shot back as he got up and lifted the homemade device that they called a bucket. It was a bottle inside another filled with water. It was the quickest way to get a massive amount of weed smoke into the body in one large blast. Better than any bong they had ever owned.

"What we gonnae dae for more weed when this runs out? Shit's changed. There isn't goin' tae be any more stuff getting shipped in, and most of the farms here have probably been destroyed." Tommy said as he expelled a cloud of smoke.

"Fuck knows, man. Probably best we go on the hunt for some before we run out. Save us being left short."

"Aye, sounds good, ma man. Ye manage tae get any o' the other lads yet?"

"Na man, mobile phone signal is still down n' so's the net."

"Fuck sake, man. One wee storm n' everything fa's apart'."

"It wisnae really a wee storm, tae be fair, mate."

"Naw, a know, but ye know what a fuckin' mean. It's like the dark ages. Actually, need tae go round somebody's house n' chap the fuckin' door. That's the kinda shit ma gran used tae have tae dae, back in the day."

Tommy and Zanda both had a chuckle at that. They were fifteen and used to being surrounded by fifteen to twenty of the boys at any given time. There was fuck all to do at the best of times in central Scotland, so they mostly stood down the woods, away from the police. Drinking and smoking was the hobby of choice, but they hadn't seen any of the boys since everything went down. Now they only had the news coming through on an old radio they had at Zanda's place. Zanda's parents were both junkies, and they hadn't been home since the storms stopped. As soon as the natural disaster had calmed down, they were out hunting for smack. Typical junkies —

always looking for a fix. Zanda had no interest in them anyway, a fact that was entirely mutual. He had brought himself up with a little help from his gran but she was gone now. Even Tommy knew how little he cared. It was a place to crash and smoke. When they were in, he was out. But the boys had just hung around for a few days, getting stoned, and waiting to see what happened next. They both expected that more of the team would've rallied around by now but nothing.

"Right, fuck this, son. C'mon, let's get out n' about n' see if we can find any o' the lads." Tommy said.

"Aye, might as well before the fuckin' junkies get it." Zanda replied.

They both left the flat with a bottle of Buckfast and a few pre-rolled joints to tide them over on their hunt for more grass.

"What about jumpin' round tae Wee Smokey's first? Cunt doesn't sell it, but his brother always has a few ounces of Dawg lying around. Maybe even some o' that Orange Crush or Single Malt," Tommy said.

"Aye man, good call."

Zanda pulled the door to the flat shut behind him. It could only be pulled over because his parents had broken the lock to get in after locking themselves out one night. Of course, it had never been fixed. There was fuck all worth stealing anyway. Zanda never left anything of value in the flat for fear that his parents would sell it to get their next hit.

As they walked down the stairs of the close, it smelt worse than usual. Everything reeked of sea air but with a rotten tinge to it. Too briny. It was almost suffocating as they got to the bottom landing and opened the large security door — another door that didn't lock. The council had gotten fed up repairing it sometime in the nineties. The boys turned right, towards the end of the street, then cut through the park. The team sometimes hung around the park, but neither thought any of the boys would be outside with everything going on and the intolerable stench.

As they walked side by side, Zanda pulled one of the joints from his jacket. The jacket was years old and a bit snug, but it was in better condition than most of his clothes. Unlike most of his mates, his parents didn't buy him the latest designer fashions and any money he made was spent on drink or weed. He never looked at himself as being like his parents. All his mates smoked and drank — the 'normal' stimulants of youth — so he was just a regular teen as he saw it. He would generally get a feed at whoever's house he was in each night or, at worst, grab a few items from the reduced-price shelf in Tesco. If you went in late enough at night, there was always decent stuff to pick from. Items that were past their sell-by-date by the time the clock struck midnight. Zanda always wondered how they worked the dates out so precisely, but it was only ever a passing thought. Most nights, he couch-surfed. No one ever got fed up with him. He was a small lad, so he didn't take up much space, and he always made everyone laugh and feel good — who doesn't welcome that? He knew that some of the acceptance was pity, though he didn't like lingering on those thoughts. He never wanted to be pitied. When he was old enough, he would get a good job and move out of his parent's dump of a flat and live a better life. Or at least, that was the plan before the UK was destroyed. Fuck knew what would happen now.

As the boys turned the corner, there was a small lane into the park. Tommy gasped and put his hand on Zanda's chest, pushing him back.

"What the fuck is it?" Zanda asked. Trying to look over his taller friend's shoulder.

"Shit. I don't want ye tae look, man, but a think it's your parents."

"Fuck, ye think a havnae found them lyin' up this lane, smashed out their tits a thousand times? Move, let's get goin'."

Tommy moved to the side to block Zanda from passing.

"Nah, man. Not like this. A think they might be deed, bro." Tommy's voice wavered. He knew they were dead but wasn't sure how to break it to his friend. Zanda was right. They probably had been lying in the lane, full of smack and passed out but something else had gotten them. They had countless slashes and cuts all over their bodies. Shredded skin hung from their faces; large patches of bone were visible. Blood had pooled out all around them but was now dried and congealed. Who knew how long they had been lying there.

"Fuck sake, move mate. Let me see them. They're likely just out o' it." Zanda shoved past Tommy. "Holy fuck! Guess they are deed." A strange feeling passed over Zanda. It wasn't sadness. It had been a long time since he had felt anything for them. They were parents by title alone. They only wanted the extra benefit money they claimed for having him. As he looked down at their shredded bodies, he realised it was relief that he felt. Relieved to be free from them. Just the association was a burden. Now he could move on with his life. He hawked up a grogger from his throat and spat on what was left of the man, the junkie — his father.

"Fuck them, mate. C'mon, let's find the boys." Zanda said.

"Mate, you aren't thinkin'. What did this tae them?" Tommy was freaked out.

"Shut up, ya dafty. They probably OD'd, and a few stray dogs have come along and had some lunch. Hopefully, they finish them off cause A'm no burying the cunts."

"A don't think that wis dogs that done that, mate. It looked like slashes."

"They likely owed some cunt money n' it's caught up wi' them. Fuck them, mate. C'mon, we've got stuff tae dae. The police will find them eventually — they can deal wi' them. They're no ma problem, son." Zanda replied, making his way into the park and leaving the bodies behind.

"You awright, mate? A know you never liked them, but they were still your maw n' da."

"They weren't ma fuckin' maw n' da. She wis an old cow that nae cunt wanted to pay for a ride anymair, n' he wis either the bam that shot his muck up her clatty hole or the cunt that came along when she wis pregnant. Nae love lost, son. Fuck, it's probably been a few year since a last spoke tae them n' that's wae us sometimes living in the same house. Best thing for them. No cunt'll miss them."

Tommy knew that Zanda was serious. He was a tough lad. Always had been. He never had much choice. Always resourceful and always the first into a fight, even if the other lads were twice his size. Some people have such a bad life that little scares them. They just don't see how things could be worse. Zanda was a good friend, loyal to the end, but he wasn't someone you would want to cross because he would get you at some point — he didn't need a team rallied around him. For a wee guy, he could go to town with the best of them. Fast, strong and he was a thinker. He was calculated in everything he did. When you learnt everything on the streets and from a younger age than most, you became wise. They had been best friends for a long time and looked out for each other, but Zanda was always tougher. Tommy knew he would struggle to deal with the loss of his parents, but they were very different. He wouldn't broach the subject again unless Zanda brought it up.

"A cannae see anybody, mate," Zanda said.

Tommy snapped out of his thoughts. "Na man, A didnae think there would be many folk wandering around. It's fuckin' stinkin' in't it?"

"Aye. Wonder how long it'll take for that smell to go?"

"Fuck knows mate. Hope it's no long, though. If we run out o' weed, everything starts tae smell even stronger."

The boys continued across the park, unaware of crabs approaching them from several different parts of the park. Tommy was unsure of what to say next. Zanda had just lit another joint and was puffing away quietly. Tommy pulled the bottle of Buckfast from his pocket and cracked it open. He necked the bottle and passed it to Zanda.

"Cheers, ma man." Zanda took a large drink. "Fuck, that hits the spot." He took another, then passed it back to Tommy along with the joint. Tommy nodded in thanks.

"Think there will be anyone in Smokey's?" Tommy asked.

"Fuck knows mate. Worth a try — if there isnae anyone there, we can take a wee jaunt roon tae Danny's. There's always some cunt in Danny's."

Tommy took another swig of wine and passed it back to Zanda but kept the joint. Zanda went to lift the bottle to his mouth but stopped short.

"Ye hear that mate?"

"What? A cannae hear anything." Tommy replied.

"Listen. Shhhh..."

Tommy stopped smoking the joint and listened. There was a sound, albeit quiet, but it was getting louder. It sounded like clicking.

"Fuck is that?" Tommy asked.

"Sounds like su'hin clickin', mate. In fact. It sounds like loads o' clicks."

Both lads turned to look behind them. At first, they couldn't see anything but the longer they looked around, they saw the grass was moving. Every so often, they would see flashes of red moving through the green.

"Mate, this is fuckin' shady. C'mon," Tommy pulled Zanda's arm.

Zanda might be tough, but he knew something was far from right here.

"Aye mate, let's get the fuck out of here. C'mon."

Zanda quickly screwed the lid on the bottle back and slipped it into his jacket. Tommy tossed the joint. As they began to run, he saw the grass around where the joint landed going wild, though he was too busy making his getaway to see what was there.

The boys sprinted across the park and vaulted the fence that surrounded it. They landed in someone's back garden but no one came out of the house to see what was going on.

"What the fuck wis that, mate?" Tommy asked.

"No idea, son, but I'm glad we got a move on. I'm gonnae have a look."

Zanda got up from the grass and jumped onto the fence so he could look over it. He was silent for a few seconds.

Tommy got up and dusted himself off. "Crabs." Zanda said.

"What did you say?"

"Crabs mate, hundreds o' the fuckers, n' no the type you find in the lassie's knickers that you run about way. Big red dodgy-looking bastards."

Tommy thought he was going nuts, so he clambered up onto the fence to see for himself. Although the park grass was overgrown, the number of crabs that were moving towards them was unbelievable. They were crawling over the top of each other to get to the fence, but the six-foot wooden fence surrounded the ground, so they couldn't get under it. The gaps between the slats were less than an inch across, there was no squeezing through either. The crabs were climbing over each other, but Zanda doubted they would make it to a six-foot mount to the top. They were still coming from all ends of the park, though, so he wouldn't have bet on it. They looked at each other and said the same thing at the same time. "Smokey's!" They jumped from the fence and jogged around the side of the house. The street was empty.

"Gies another drink o' the wine, mate."

Zanda took the bottle from his jacket and passed it over. He sparked a joint while Tommy took a gulp then passed it back.

"Just finish it mate."

Zanda upended the bottle and drank what was left.

"Fuckin' needed that. Can you believe that shit?" He passed the joint to Tommy and they started walking again.

"Na man. I seen it, but it wis mental. Where the fuck did a' the crabs come from? Dae ye think they're here because o' the tsunami?"

"Must be mate."

The boys walked at a fast pace towards the end of the street. Rather than taking the long way round, they jumped the back gardens of a few houses and got to Smokey's. Tommy was first to the door. He gave it a few quick, hard knocks, then stood back. The house seemed quiet. Zanda scanned the windows for any movement. Nothing.

"Fuck me. I'm no fit enough for a' this shit," Tommy said.

"A know mate. It's brutal. Am fucked. Half a bottle o' wine n' a few joints in ye disnae help matters." Zanda said. They burst into fits of hysterics. After everything that had happened over the last seven days and then being chased by the crabs, coupled with the drink and marijuana, they both just let go. They were doubled over when they heard it again. Click! Click! Click!

Tommy was facing Zanda and saw easily a hundred crabs clicking their way towards them as they scuttled between each other.

"Fuck this man. Danny's house. C'mon!" Zanda grabbed Tommy's arm, pulling him into action. The two sprinted from Smokey's gate and ran.

"Where the fuck are they coming from?" Tommy panted.

Zanda didn't answer. He just looked at Tommy as they ran, hoping he and his old friend would make it to safety. The crab clicking didn't quieten as they fled. How fast did they move? Why were they chasing them? Did crabs really attack people? Did they hunt in packs? He had no answers to the questions. He rarely attended school, and there was no television or internet in his flat. He was streetwise but knew fuck all about crabs.

"This way, son," Tommy said, cutting up a lane that would take them closer to Danny's. As they ran into the next street, they heard a scream to their left, an old lady and (presumably) her granddaughter were screaming their lungs out at the edge of a garden. The boys had no idea why they were outside. They could only watch as crabs swarmed the pair, stripping the flesh from their bodies. Zanda started to run towards them, but Tommy grabbed him.

"They're gone, mate, n' look." Tommy nodded down the lane, where their own flood of crabs was entering.

"Fuck!" Zanda yelled. He looked back as the woman and child fell to the ground, and the crabs swept over them; a bloody crustaceous tsunami. By the time he turned to sprint the other way down the street with Tommy, he couldn't see an inch of flesh. The crabs operated like piranha, attacking in groups, stripping the flesh from bones in less than a minute. The boys kept up a fast pace and began jumping through gardens again, hoping the crabs would struggle with some of the fences. They knew the schemes like the backs of their hands. They had grown up jumping the same fences to evade the police. They moved with expert agility, even though neither of them was particularly sporty.

As they jumped the last fence, they got to Danny's street. They were just about to run towards his house when they heard a mass of crabs rounding the corner.

"That cannae be the same fuckers as before, is it?" Tommy panted, breathlessly.

"Does it matter? Run for Danny's or dive over more back gardens?"

"A say Danny's mate. Am runnin' out o' steam n' they are coming fae everywhere."

"Sound. Race ye." Zanda grinned and burst into a sprint.

Tommy couldn't help but chuckle as he chased after him. Zanda had always been wild and always seemed to find the humour in the worst of situations. As they sprinted towards

Danny's place, a larger group of crabs came from the other side of the street. They moved slower but the boys were trapped.

"Fuck dae we dae noo, man?" Tommy asked.

"What the fuck dae we always dae, son? Go down fuckin' swingin'." With that, Zanda ran to one of the four-foot wooden fences and kicked it apart. He pulled off one of the slats and threw it to Tommy, then pulled himself one free. They were fairly solid and had nails sticking out. It was the best they could do, all things considered.

Zanda turned to Tommy. "You know a love ye, ya cunt! Ye always treated me the same as every other cunt, never looked doon at me."

"Shut up, ya dick. Don't get a' fuckin' soft oan us noo. We've got about two hunner o' these crab bastards tae kill n' you want tae have a heart tae heart. That's too much o' the old wine, ma son."

Zanda laughed heartily. "We always did say tae the end, eh?"

"Sure did, ma man. Right. Ye ready tae fuck these things up? Back tae back n' just go for it?"

"Aye! Fuckin' right a am. Airdrie Young Team Ya Cunts!" Zanda screamed at the top of his voice and started swinging his weapon at the closest crabs. Tommy was at his back doing the same. What a fucking way tae go. Zanda thought. Fuckin' munched down like a Chinese meal by a bunch o' fuckin' crabs. His adrenaline was kicking in now. This was where everything would go red, and he would lose his shit — when suddenly he heard a shout.

"A Y Fuckin' T, ya wee red crab pussies!"

Followed by another.

"C'mon then! Ya fishy wee pricks!"

And another.

"Who are ye! Who are ye! Who are ye!"

Then all hell let loose. Upstairs windows of the two up, two down flats started to open as other lads from the young team piled out into the street. They were armed with samurai swords, baseball bats, cleavers, and other weapons that most young teams had stored away somewhere. Petrol bombs flew from windows and landed amongst the crabs, setting several on fire and scattering others. The other lads included Smokey, his big brother Tam, Danny and a few of the younger ones — Barry, Wullie Nae Nose, Eddie, and a few boys that Zanda had never seen. The team swarmed the crabs that were trying to skedaddle as more petrol bombs flew. Large sections of the street were on fire. The team gathered towards each other as they killed the last few crabs that had hung around while the others had scarpered. As the brief but fierce war came to an end, Zanda and Tommy dropped onto their asses, exhausted.

"Fuck sake, lads, ye should've phoned ahead n' we coulda looked out for ye. Looked like ye's were struggling there." Big Tam said.

Zanda started laughing, then Tommy joined him.

"You know the phones are doon, ya cunt!"

"Aye, just fuckin' wae yous. C'mon, get yer arses up intae the hoose. We have a tonne o' swally n' fuckin' ounces o' weed n' ching, lads. Let's get in n' get the party started before these wee red cunts team up again."

Tam reached out and took Zanda's hand and one from Tommy and pulled them both to their feet. "Fair play lads, ye's fair stood yer fuckin ground. Don't think ye were gonnae win that one, though."

Zanda looked thoughtful for a minute and looked around at big Tam. "Naw, you're probably right there. A 'hink they woulda got us eventually, but if a did die, a'd 'ave been straight roon tae see yer old maw n' gi' her a good seeing tae."

Tam burst into laughter, and punched Zanda a solid jab in the arm.

"Ya wee dick, ye. Always did like ye, ya cunt." He paused for a second and then roared, "Who are we?" This started a chant from all around them and from the windows.

"A.Y.T! A.Y.T! A.Y.T! A.Y.T! A.Y.T!"

The End

Those Damn Trees
By
David Sodergren

"They're getting closer," said Margaret.

Tom Campbell looked up from his morning paper. His wife hovered by the kitchen window, her hands fidgeting across the worktop.

"Eh?" he said, in no mood for conversation.

She turned to him, a worried look creasing her face. "The trees." She broke into an unconvincing smile. "If I didn't know better, I'd swear they were..."

"I don't want to hear it," Tom interrupted. "First the cows were looking at you funny, then it was too quiet at night. Now it's bloody *sentient trees.*" He raised his paper and shook his head. "Get a grip, Margaret."

He watched her over the top of the broadsheet. She turned back to the window, the sunlight streaming over her face, making it glow a serene yellow. From upstairs came the sound of small feet thudding across the floor.

"Nicky!" shouted Tom. "Keep it down! It's half eight in the bloody morning."

"He's just a child," said Margaret, though when he looked at her, she was still staring out the window. "Tom," she said.

"What now?"

Couldn't a man get any peace in his own house? Was he doomed to be forever interrupted from his morning ritual?

"Someone's coming," she said.

"Oh, aye. The fucking trees, I suppose, on their way to sell us some encyclopedias."

She tore her eyes from the window and stared at him. "No.

It's *them.*"

Tom nodded, folded his paper, and pushed his chair back from the table with a screech.

"Stay here," he sighed. "I'll get the shotgun."

He opened the door before they had the chance to knock. There were three of them this time, three men impeccably attired in identical, neatly pressed suits. One of them shuffled forwards holding a briefcase, an insincere smile etched on his face. When he spotted the shotgun cradled in Tom's hands, he hesitated.

"Mr. Campbell," he said. "Pleased to meet you. I'm—"

"Dinnae give a shite what your name is," said Tom. "You're not welcome here."

The man started to open the briefcase, his nervous fingers clumsily fumbling with the latches. Beads of sweat trickled down his forehead.

"Mr. Campbell, please, I'm sure we can come to an arrangement. I have a new offer from Mr. Robbins, and I think you'll find it quite agreeable."

Tom took a deep breath. "How many times have I told you wee arseholes that I'm not selling my fucking land?"

"A number of times, I believe."

"Do I need to get it tattooed on my face?"

"That won't be necessary, Mr.—"

"Then why are you still here? Why are you bothering my family?"

"But Mr. Campbell, this new offer is significantly higher than—"

Tom raised the shotgun and pointed both barrels into the man's chest.

"Get the fuck off my property and don't come back. This land has been in my family for centuries, and I'll be damned if I'll sell it to some cunts to build a bunch of student flats."

"Not flats," said one of the other men, bravely stepping forward. "This is prime space for an outdoor retail experience and—"

"Fuck off!" roared Tom, thumbing the safety on the shotgun. They backed off, and when he fired into the air they turned tail and scurried back to their car, tripping over each other in their haste.

"You'll regret this," one of them shouted as he scrambled into the vehicle and slammed the door. Black fumes belched from the exhaust pipe as the wheels skidded in the dirt, and then they were off, careening through the thick forest. Tom watched them leave with a wry grin.

Funny.

From where he was standing, the trees *did* look closer.

For Tom, that was the last day when things still felt normal. The men never returned, and life lumbered inexorably on, but something was up with Margaret. Nicky, of course, never noticed. What can you expect from a four-year-old? His life was all naps, Paw Patrol, and shitting himself. To him, the acres of forest that surrounded the property were a giant playground, nothing more, nothing less. But to Tom, they had taken on a sinister aspect. He blamed Margaret. Her behaviour was becoming irrational.

One morning, he came down the stairs in his slippers and dressing gown to find her standing in the doorway, her hands gripping the frame with white knuckles. When he touched her shoulder, she jumped.

"Good grief, woman," he said. "You're on edge."

She looked away from him, but not quickly enough. He could see the red around her eyes from where she had been crying.

"It's so quiet," she said.

"Aye," smiled Tom. "That's why we moved here, remember? To get some bloody peace."

She stared out across the land, land that had become theirs when Tom's father had passed away two years ago. "But it's *too* quiet."

"Oh, come on! You—"

She looked at him, eyes wide and frightened. "Listen!" she hissed. "Just *listen.*"

He did. "What am I listening for?"

"For anything. Don't you understand? There's nothing. No sound at all. You hear any birds, or animals?"

"Never been one for nature," he said with a shrug. He placed a hand on her arm, and she wriggled free.

"Those damn trees," she muttered, brushing past him and creeping back inside. Something about the way she moved bothered him.

It was as if she were afraid the trees were watching.

Nicky went missing the following day. When the call from Margaret came through, Tom was busy flirting with the office secretary, leaning over the desk and trying to peek down her blouse.

"It's Nicky," Margaret had sobbed over the phone, her voice frantic. "He's gone! I can't find him!"

The words rang in Tom's ears as he raced his car down the single lane country road, the trees whipping by in a frenzy of greens and browns. The sky was grey, leaden with clouds that threatened to burst. He took the turnoff past the loch and followed the road that led towards the mountain, at the base of which sat his ancestral home, so perfect in its sombre isolation. The heavens opened, the deluge turning the dirt track into a thick brown sludge.

Gnarled branches clattered against the windshield. The willows drooped low, heavy with rainfall, his windscreen wipers struggling to keep up. Tom flicked on his full beams to penetrate the darkness, the canopy of trees refusing to allow any light through.

He emerged into the clearing, into the daylight. A figure in red hurried towards him, slipping in the mud.

"Margaret," he shouted as he threw the door open, running to her.

She gazed into his eyes, her red sweater soaked through. "They took him," she said.

"Who... those men?"

She shook her head, her wet hair flicking against her cheeks.

"No," she said, her breath coming in tight gasps. She gripped his arms and wept. "It was the trees."

"Margaret, please, you—"

She regarded him with crazed, tormented eyes, and grabbed him by the lapels of the wet shirt that clung to his body.

"The trees took my baby!" she screamed.

Tom stood before the forest. He felt no fear in the presence of the great trees. Margaret was being absurd. It wasn't the first time Nicky had gotten lost in the woods. On the last occasion, Tom had found him playing by the fallen pine tree barely twenty feet into the woods. He was four and couldn't get far on his stumpy wee legs.

"Nicky!" he shouted, casting his torchlight between the trunks. The light made the shadows move, but Tom was a pragmatic man. Margaret's belief in occult bollocks like astrology had initially drawn him to her, her carefree nature the opposite of the boardroom stiffs he worked alongside. But he had assumed motherhood would have knocked that nonsense out of her head, not made matters worse.

He brushed aside some branches, snapping a glistening gossamer spiderweb.

"Nicky!"

No response.

"I'm not angry, I promise," he lied. "Just come home. Your mother's worried sick."

He crossed the perimeter and entered the forest. A deadening, curious silence greeted him. He headed towards the fallen tree, where he himself had whiled away countless hours as a child, climbing up the trunk, pretending it was a pirate ship, clinging on to the make-believe mast.

But now it wasn't there.

Impossible, he thought. *It's been there as long as this house has stood.*

He walked further, questioning his memory. Something caught his eye, a glimpse of royal blue through the branches that entwined unnaturally and forced him to duck his head to pass. He squeezed uncomfortably between two trees. Had he put on weight? Perhaps. Working a desk job could do that to you.

He crouched, reaching for the blue object. It was one of Nicky's action figures, an anthropomorphized dog wearing a policeman's hat. So, he *had* been here. That was good. He glanced up, and there was the downed pine tree, still sitting at its forty-five-degree angle, the bark white and dead, the roots bursting angrily from the earth. Something was different, though.

Something was off.

The trunk bulged, a circular mound protruding grotesquely near the top like a rodent caught in a snake's belly. Tom took a step closer, placing his palm against the bulge.

It was warm.

"What the fuck," said Tom, and then something inside the tree lashed out, the dull thud reverberating for miles across the silent forest. Startled, Tom fell backwards, watching as the trunk split, hot blood oozing from the cracks like sap, pooling on the ground and steaming in the misty, frozen air.

"Daddy!" came a shrill cry, but by then, Tom was hurtling through the forest, the branches lashing his face, reaching for him, trying to curl around his arms, his neck... and then he was in the clearing, breaking free of their grasp and collapsing on the sodden grass. He looked back to where he had come from, at the trees curling around each other, slithering into obscene knots, their bark splintering and raining to the ground.

Tom turned and ran for the house. He needed a drink.

"Where's the police?" said Margaret. She paced back and forth, biting her nails. "I called them hours ago."

Tom had no answer.

Margaret stopped by the window.

"They're getting closer," she murmured, her voice tremulous.

"Don't be ridiculous," said Tom, already on his fourth brandy. He hadn't told her about the tree, because he no longer believed he had seen it.

Trees didn't *bleed.* They didn't cry out, and certainly not in the childish voice of his missing son.

That's right, he told himself. *Now drink up.*

"It's those men," said Margaret. "Call them, Tom. Call them and tell them you'll sell. Nicky might still be... they might have him somewhere.... they..."

She trailed off, gazing through the rain-streaked pane.

"The police will be here soon," said Tom. His brandy glass was empty. He tottered to the cabinet and opened it. As he lifted the bottle, he spied a thin green weed curled in the corner. Eyeing it with distaste, he tore it out and stamped it underfoot, grinding the plant beneath his heel.

Outside, the wind whipped through the trees, making it sound like they were screaming. Tom closed his eyes and drank straight from the bottle.

"The police will be here soon," he repeated, as Margaret put her forehead against the glass and quietly wept.

The police never arrived. Tom lifted the receiver of the phone in the hallway and started to dial.

The line was dead.

He staggered drunkenly up the stairs to the bedroom. It was almost ten. He entered to find Margaret hurriedly stuffing clothes into a small suitcase.

"Where the devil do you think you're going?" he slurred.

"I can't stay here," she replied without looking at him, closing the suitcase and pressing the lid down. "I'm going to drive into town. I'll speak to the police myself."

"And where are you planning on staying?"

She zipped the case up and stared at him. "Anywhere but

here." She sounded small, frightened. "If Nicky comes back, will you—"

"You're acting like a fool," he snapped. "There's nothing out there."

She glared at him. "Then why aren't you out there looking for him? Why are you hiding in here with me? Your son is missing, and you're—"

"If he comes back, I'll call you." He just wanted her out of his house. A headache gnawed at his temples, and he wondered idly — not for the first time — whether Nicky actually *was* his son, or the offspring of that college lecturer he always thought Margaret had fancied.

His wife brushed past him, lugging the suitcase to the door. She stopped and turned to face him.

"Come with me, Tom," she said. "It's not safe here."

He sat down heavily on the bed. "If... *when* he comes back, I'll call you."

She didn't reply. He watched her leave, listening to her footsteps on the stairs. The front door slammed shut, then an engine grumbled into life.

Tom lay back and let sleep overcome him.

When he woke, it was morning. He shook his groggy head and coughed. Something scratched irritatingly in his throat, and the light hurt his eyes. He got out of bed, still wearing yesterday's clothes, and reached for the shutters.

"Fucking impossible," he whispered, his hands dropping to his sides.

The trees weren't just closer. They were right outside his yard, the white wooden fence buckling against their mighty trunks. They must have moved fifty feet overnight.

"You're still drunk," he said, but he knew he wasn't.

He backed away slowly, his heel nudging the empty brandy bottle. His throat tickled him like he had smoked a twenty deck the night before. Something was caught in there. He marched to the en suite bathroom and leaned against the wall, looking at his haggard reflection in the mirror. Opening his mouth, he peered down his throat.

He gagged when he saw it.

There was a plant in there, thin and green. He reached two trembling fingers in, the weed recoiling from his grasp. It was wrapped around his tonsils.

Heart hammering, he yanked open a drawer and rummaged inside until he found the tweezers.

"Get out of my mouth, you wee cunt," he said, opening wide and reaching in. The tiny pincers jabbed at the back of his throat. He placed them around the stem of the weed. It writhed angrily, winding its way over his hand, moving with alarming speed. Tom reflexively jerked the blades closed. He winced in agony as they caught his tonsils, cutting them. He spat into the sink, the weed splattering against the porcelain alongside his own blood.

There was a knock at the front door.

"Fuck off," he gargled, dropping the tweezers into the sink and running from the bathroom. Grabbing his shotgun, he jogged down the stairs to the hallway. Blood trickled down his chin. He walked to the front door, grabbed the handle, and threw it open.

There was nothing there. The trees were in his yard now, their branches swaying languidly. Margaret's red coat dangled from one of them, the fabric shredded.

Aside from the cool morning breeze, all was silent.

Tom stepped cautiously over the threshold; the shotgun heavy in his tired hands. He spat a mouthful of blood onto the grass.

"Come on then," he said. "What're you waiting for?"

Nothing happened.

He stepped forward and snatched Margaret's jacket from the branch. It was wet with blood, the trees regarding him with the cruel indifference of nature. He pointed his shotgun at the nearest one and fired, the trunk exploding in a shower of bark. Suddenly the branches were alive, whipping around like fire hoses, lashing across his exposed face and arms, wrenching the shotgun from his hands. Tom threw himself backwards, the branches following like obscene, groping tentacles. He slammed the front door, trapping one of the branches. Still, it writhed, striking out towards him. More plants sprouted between the cracks of the door, edging their way in. The door started to warp, a thick branch bursting through the letterbox like a twisted jack-in-the-box.

Tom scrambled to his feet and ran for the basement, skidding on the expensive John Lewis rug Margaret had wasted his money on. The whole house seemed to shrink as the trees closed in. Wood splintered, glass shattering all around. Tom opened the basement door and tumbled helplessly down the stairs.

There were no windows here. No way in.

And no way out.

That didn't matter. He pulled a cord, a single bare light bulb illuminating the interior, and hastened to his workbench. There, hanging above the selection of scattered tools, was what he needed.

His Stiga SP 426 chainsaw.

"Come to papa," he muttered, lifting it reverentially from its shelf, cradling the powerful tool like a baby. Loose debris rained down around him from the ceiling, the house shrieking.

He laid the chainsaw down and snapped off the leg from a chair he had been reupholstering, wrapping an oily rag around it.

"This is my fucking house," he said, lighting the rag, half-closing his eyes as the chair leg erupted into a vicious blaze.

The basement door split down the centre. The trees were inside the house. Tom opened the throttle of the chainsaw and tugged on the chain. After a couple of pulls, it roared in fury.

The branches were slithering down the stairs.

In one hand, Tom held the torch. In the other, the chainsaw. It purred contentedly in his demented grip.

"Come on then, you bastards," he growled. "Fucking have at it."

He started up the steps. The branches moved back, the heat from the torch keeping them at bay. Tom stomped into the hallway. Two pine trees blocked his escape, their roots churning against the floorboards like oversized maggots. He waved the torch before him, but they remained in place.

"Get the fuck out of my way!"

He lunged towards the nearest tree, holding the torch to it. It screamed.

The damn tree *screamed* as it went up in flames.

Two burning branches reached out to him. Tom batted them away, then ploughed the whirring chainsaw into the reedy trunk. Amber sap gushed out in a torrent, hot and bubbling, spraying over Tom, the walls, the floor. He withdrew the blade, then plunged it in again. With a loud crack, the trunk broke, the tree toppling over into the second one, bringing it to the ground.

Tom set them ablaze and hopped over the fiery remains, heading for the door. The wail of the trees pierced his ears, drowning out even the savage fury of the chainsaw motor.

He reached the front door and stopped; his passage blocked. Dozens of branches formed an impenetrable web across the exit. And there, tangled amongst them, was his wife.

Margaret.

Her clothes had been stripped from her body. Branches penetrated her flesh. Her breasts, her torso, her legs, even a couple of smaller ones through her face. One disappeared up her nostril, another through the torn skin of her cheek.

She gazed at him through soft, lifeless eyes, her body red with her own blood.

"Help me," she mouthed at him.

Tom stared at her in disbelief. "Fuck that," he said.

He raised the chainsaw and brought it down on Margaret's shoulder. She threw her head back and cried as the spinning blade cut through her skin, making short work of the thin bones. Blood fountained across the room as Tom kept cutting. He angled the saw towards her crotch, the branches that held her powerless to withstand the awesome force of the power tool.

Margaret was dead by the time her belly opened, and her steaming guts flooded the floor. As she split fully in two, Tom stepped over the heap of viscera that had once been his wife and left the house.

The trees formed a circle around him, but they didn't dare come closer. Still, he had to hurry. The torch wouldn't last forever, and he wasn't sure how much fuel remained in the saw. He jogged towards where he knew the road to be, following the peak of the distant mountain. As long as he headed in the direction of Cook's Point, he would find the road.

The trees circled him, trying to confuse him. Was that possible?

They're trying to kill you. Anything's possible, you daft shite.

The torch wasn't strong enough to dispel the darkness, but it kept it at bay. Tom broke into a jog, the roots of the trees scurrying alongside him like millions of spider legs. He saw lights ahead, red and blue flashing monotonously.

The police car. He passed by, the occupants of the vehicle torn apart and splattered across the interior. The window had been smashed, and the remains of one cop dribbled pathetically down the side of the panda car.

Tom moved on.

A pinecone struck him in the face. He winced. Another hit him, then another, launched with such velocity that he felt blood trickling from a gash in his forehead. He swung the torch, trying not to think of just how insane his current situation was.

"Fuck off," he said as he strode onwards, hoping he was walking in the right direction. Sure enough, the trees parted for the first time since he left the house. He saw the moon glimmering off the gentle ripples of the loch, and ran to the water, wading into it, drenching his trouser legs. He splashed along the bank, heading for the old boathouse. The trees kept pace with him.

Tom raised the torch as a warning, and at that moment — with the perfect timing of a Scottish summer — it started to rain.

The trees closed in as the torch flickered and died.

Two birch trees seemed to lunge for him. Tom swung the saw in an arc, slicing them in half. The tool slipped from his grasp and disappeared into the water. Tom turned from the trees and dived into the loch, keeping below the surface, pulling himself along by the rocks below him. When he bumped his shoulder off a support beam, he surfaced to find himself in the boathouse, the rain drumming off the corrugated tin roof.

"Can't catch me," he sneered desperately, clambering into one of the two fishing boats, nearly capsizing it. The boathouse shook. Wood smashed, falling in around him as he untied the rope that moored the boat to the thin walkway.

He pushed off from the pier as an enormous Douglas fir wrenched the boathouse roof apart, towering over him in all its hellish majesty.

"Aye, come and get me, you fucking wanker," grinned Tom. He gripped the oars and worked them hard, not stopping until the boat rocked gently in the centre of the loch. He looked at the trees leering impotently on the edge of the water. "Fucking wee pricks," he laughed, his whole body trembling with adrenaline. He dropped the anchor and waited for his breathing to slow.

Now there was nothing to do but wait.

Tom's eyes flickered open. It took him a few seconds to remember why he was lying in a boat in the middle of the loch. Had it been a dream? Had it fuck! He wiped blood from his face and sat up stiffly. Row boats were not designed for comfortable sleeping, he decided.

The sun was setting, spreading its golden-red light across the sky.

Red sky at night, shepherds' delight, he heard his mum say. He looked over to the shore. The trees were gone. Had they given up? Was it over? He thought it best to row the other direction and head into town. No sense in taking any chances. First, though, he had business to attend to — his aching bladder. He stood carefully and unzipped his fly, then pissed over the side of the boat, the gentle splash of the water pleasing to his ears.

The stream cut off abruptly.

He looked down at his cock, then screamed wretchedly as pain wracked his genitals, coursing through his body. He collapsed into the boat, making it rock from side-to-side. His penis jerked with a life of its own, rearing up like a cobra. Something green emerged from the tip.

A plant.

"No!" he cried, reaching for it. His dick moved to the side, avoiding his fingers. The plant emerged further. It was getting thicker. He felt like his cock might burst. He tried to grasp it again, then noticed the thin green veins emerging from beneath his fingernails. His thumbnail cracked as a vine erupted out, but Tom didn't notice.

The pressure in his skull was too great.

Something slithered through his guts, heading up his throat and scratching his insides raw. He put his hands to his ears, feeling the ferns that sprouted there tickle his palms. His neck bulged as something pressed against it, trying to get out, and then his vision was gone, his eyeballs popping wetly, two glistening red flowers blossoming from his ruined sockets.

His last thought was of that bottle of brandy from the previous evening.

Margaret had always told him he should drink less.

He tried to laugh, but the movement forced the sapling through his stretched jugular in an eruption of gore, and then Tom Campbell was no more.

Tristan Robbins stood with his arms crossed, smiling as the diggers fired into life. He clutched the blueprints for the retail complex in one sweaty hand. It was more for show than anything — he was a businessman, not an architect — but several journalists were coming today, and he needed to look important.

As the house that once belonged to Tom Campbell shuddered from the impact of the wrecking ball, Robbins' grin grew even wider. He couldn't believe the serum had worked as well as it had. He really ought to give Pierce, his chief scientist, a raise. Well, maybe not a raise, but at least a bonus. He motioned to the man, who walked over, the hardhat balancing precariously on his curly brown hair.

"You did good, Pierce," said Robbins. "I have a few friends overseas who could put your serum to good use."

"Military application?" asked Pierce.

Robbins nodded. His smile faltered, and he looked intently at Pierce. "You sure we're safe here?"

Pierce chuckled. "Absolutely. The effects last a maximum of one week."

"You ever tried it on a human subject?"

Pierce shuddered. "Yeah. Best not to talk about that. It's almost lunchtime."

Robbins smiled. He could see the TV news van coming up the road. He straightened his hard hat and adjusted his tie. Years of planning were finally nearing fruition. It had cost Robbins a lot to buy off the local council and the forestry commission, but soon it would all be worth it.

When the press arrived, Robbins offered them his usual facile soundbites about 'retail-led lifestyle districts', and then it was time for photos. Robbins ushered Pierce out of the way, replacing him with a pretty seventeen-year-old in a high-legged blue swimsuit and silver tiara. Helen Lamb was the winner of this year's Miss Badenoch & Strathspey contest, and she was there because Robbins knew that a glimpse of teenage cleavage was as good a way as any to get folk excited about his new retail development.

He helped Helen adjust her satin sash, letting his fingers linger against her skin as the photographer set up the shot, and then the pair posed in front of the forest, each holding one end of a vintage crosscut saw many years past its glory days. The wind whistled through the trees behind them.

"How about a shot of you cutting a tree down?" suggested the photographer, a bearded man who looked no older than Helen. "And hurry, we're losing light." He shook his head. "Those damn trees," he muttered.

Robbins and the girl got into position. They raised the saw, holding the blade to the tree. Helen struggled with the weight, in danger of toppling over, while Robbins mugged for the camera, giving the lens his widest smile.

"Those cameras rolling?" he asked. When he received a nod of confirmation, he launched into his prepared speech. "I, Tristan Robbins, hereby christen this the very first tree to make way for The Robbins Nest, the Highlands' premier Relaxation, and Retail Therapy Complex." The photographer started snapping pictures as Robbins pulled the saw towards him, the teeth grinding against the trunk.

The tree screamed.

Robbins looked up at it. He glanced at Pierce, but the scientist was already backing away, his face ashen.

"Did you hear that?" he started to say, and then Helen Lamb screamed as a rogue branch punctured Robbins' chest, emerging with his still-beating heart impaled on the tip.

The other trees followed its lead.

They moved with an aching weariness, remembering the

way the people had treated them over the centuries; chopping them down, burning them, carving symbols into their hard skin.

The trees had lived long lives.

They had a lot of time to think.

And they were very, very angry.

The End

Thank you

I'd like to thank everyone that has given this book a read. There aren't a whole lot of horror authors in Scotland so it was nice to get some of them together for this project. If you can find the time, please consider leaving us a review on Amazon, Goodreads, or anywhere else you can think of. If you'd like a chat, you will find us on Facebook most days.

Kevin J. Kennedy

About the author's

Bill Davidson is a novelist of horror, fantasy and thrillers, based on the East Coast of Scotland. His published works include The Orangerie, The King of the Crows, The Story of Life, Cauldhame, and the Patience of the Dead, plus his collection of strange and unsettling short stories, New Gods, Old Monsters.

He has placed over 100 short stories with good publications around the world including Ellen Datlow's highly regarded Best Horror of the Year Anthology, Flame Tree, and of course Woman's Own. (He says you have to remove the axe murderers to get published in Woman's Own, and they take a dim view of cannibals)

You can find him on Facebook or billdavidsonwriting.com

John McNee is a Scottish writer of strange and disturbing horror stories.

He is known for the books PRINCE OF NIGHTMARES, GRUDGE PUNK and PETROLEUM PRECINCT, as well as his short story collection, JOHN MCNEE'S DOOM CABARET.

He can easily be found on Facebook, Twitter and YouTube, where he hosts the horror-themed cooking show A RECIPE FOR NIGHTMARES.

Kevin J. Kennedy is a horror author, editor, and anthologist. He is also the owner of KJK Publishing and he runs the bestselling 'The Horror Collection' series.' He is the author of Halloween Land, and The Clown.

He lives in the heart of Scotland with his beautiful wife, three cats, Carlito, Ariel and Luna, and a Pomchi called Orko. He can be found on Facebook if you want to chat with him.

David Sodergren lives in Scotland with his wife Heather and his best friend, Boris the Pug.

Growing up, he was the kind of kid who collected rubber skeletons and lived for horror movies. Not much has changed since then.

His best known books include the gory and romantic fairy tale The Haar, the blood-drenched folk-horror Maggie's Grave, and the analog-horror fever dream Rotten Tommy. David also writes under the pseudonym Carl John Lee, publishing splatterpunk novels such as Psychic Teenage Bloodbath and Cannibal Vengeance.

Printed in Great Britain
by Amazon